PUFFIN BOOKS

DIARY OF A WIMPY KID

BOOKS BY JEFF KINNEY

Diary of a Wimpy Kid

Diary of a Wimpy Kid: Rodrick Rules

Diary of a Wimpy Kid: The Last Straw

Diary of a Wimpy Kid: Dog Days

Diary of a Wimpy Kid: The Ugly Truth

Diary of a Wimpy Kid: Cabin Fever

Diary of a Wimpy Kid: The Third Wheel

Diary of a Wimpy Kid: Hard Luck

Diary of a Wimpy Kid: The Long Haul

The Wimpy Kid Do-It-Yourself Book

The Wimpy Kid Movie Diary

COMING SOON

More *Diary of a Wimpy Kid*

DIARY
of a
Wimpy Kid

OLD SCHOOL

by Jeff Kinney

PUFFIN

PUFFIN BOOKS

UK | USA | Canada | Ireland | Australia
India | New Zealand | South Africa

Puffin Books is part of the Penguin Random House group of companies whose
addresses can be found at global.penguinrandomhouse.com.

puffinbooks.com

First published in the English language in the USA by Amulet Books, an imprint of ABRAMS, 2015
Original English title: *Diary of a Wimpy Kid: Old School*
(All rights reserved in all countries by Harry N. Abrams, Inc.)
Published simultaneously in Great Britain by Puffin Books 2015
001

Book design by Jeff Kinney
Cover design by Chad W. Beckerman and Jeff Kinney

The moral right of the author/illustrator has been asserted

Printed in Great Britain by Clays Ltd, St Ives plc

A CIP catalogue record for this book is available from the British Library

HARDBACK
ISBN: 978-0-141-36472-8

INTERNATIONAL HARDBACK
ISBN: 978-0-141-36509-1

TO DAD

SEPTEMBER

<u>Saturday</u>

Grown-ups are always talking about the "good old days" and how things were so much better when THEY were kids.

But I think they're just jealous because MY generation has all this fancy technology and stuff they didn't have growing up.

Believe me, I'm sure when I have kids of my own I'm gonna be the exact same way my parents are NOW.

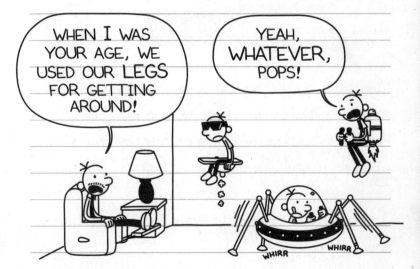

Mom's always saying that when SHE was younger it was great because everybody in town knew everybody else and it was like one giant family.

But that doesn't sound so great to ME. I like my privacy, and I really don't need everyone knowing my personal business.

Mom says the problem with society these days is that everybody's got their nose in a screen and nobody takes the time to get to know the people who live around them.

I don't really see eye to eye with Mom on that issue, though.

Personally, I think a little separation is a GOOD thing.

Lately, Mom's been going around town with a petition to get people to stop using their phones and electronic gadgets for forty-eight hours.

Mom needs a hundred signatures before she can take the petition to the town hall, but she's having trouble getting people to put their names on it.

I'm just hoping she gives up on this idea soon, because it's kind of exhausting for the rest of us to pretend we don't know her.

I really don't understand why Mom thinks we need to go BACKWARDS, anyway. From what I can tell, the old days weren't that much fun.

If you think about it, you never see anyone in those black-and-white photos SMILING.

In the old days, people were just a whole lot TOUGHER than they are today.

But human beings have EVOLVED, and now we need things like electric toothbrushes and shopping malls and soft-serve ice cream to survive.

I bet our ancestors would be pretty disappointed with the way we turned out. But once somebody invented air-conditioning there really was no turning back.

We've got so spoiled that pretty soon we won't even have to leave our homes if we don't want to.

In fact, the way we're headed, I'll bet a thousand years from now human beings won't even have SPINES.

SLITHER

Some people complain that all this technology has made us soft. But, if you ask me, that's not necessarily a BAD thing.

There are all SORTS of luxuries nowadays that make people's lives better. Take baby wipes, for example. People were using regular toilet paper for hundreds of years, and then all of a sudden some genius came up with an idea that was a total game changer.

Freshies

What really amazes me is that it took so LONG
for people to come up with the idea. I seriously
can't believe the guy who invented the light bulb
didn't see baby wipes coming.

And who KNOWS what crazy thing someone's
gonna come up with next to make our lives easier.
Whatever it is, though, I'll be the first in line to
buy it.

But if Mom had HER way we'd be living like people
did before there were computers and phones and
baby wipes.

And I really don't want to imagine living in a
world without baby wipes.

<u>Sunday</u>

Dad says that when HE was growing up, in the summertime, kids played outside all day until they got called home for dinner at night.

Well, that's pretty much the OPPOSITE of the way MY summer went this year.

I spent July and August at Film Camp, where all I did was watch movies in an air-conditioned cinema for eight hours a day.

The main reason I signed up for Film Camp was because I thought it was for people who are SERIOUS about movies, like ME.

But I found out it was REALLY just a place where parents could dump their kids off for some cheap babysitting.

The downside of spending that much time in a dark cinema is that at the end of the day it took half an hour for my eyes to adjust to the sunlight.

The other reason I signed up for Film Camp was to get out of the HOUSE. Ever since we got a pet pig, it hasn't been a lot of fun being home. Especially not at DINNER.

For the record, I think it's a TERRIBLE idea letting the pig eat at the table, because it ALREADY thinks it's a human being. And the last thing we need is for it to think it's on equal footing with the rest of us.

Right after we got the pig, Mom thought it would be fun to teach it some tricks. So she would give the pig a cookie when it stood on its hind legs.

But the pig learned to WALK like that, and it hasn't been on all fours ever since. To make matters WORSE, my little brother, Manny, put a pair of his shorts on the pig, so now it's like we're living in the house with a Disney character.

WOBBLE WOBBLE

Mom used to take the pig outside, but after it started walking upright it decided it was too good for its leash.

WAVE

Mom was worried that if the pig ran off we'd never find it, so she got a collar with one of those GPS tracking chips in it.

But, every time Mom put the collar on the pig, within five minutes it would be back OFF. And don't even ask me how the pig did THAT, since pigs don't even have THUMBS.

So now the pig just comes and goes as it pleases, and who KNOWS where it spends its time. What really stinks is that I have a curfew but the pig DOESN'T.

I think giving the pig too many privileges is a
REALLY bad idea. One day pigs will rule the
world, and it'll be my family's fault for starting
it all.

I wouldn't really have an issue with the pig if
it didn't interfere with MY life. But I was late
on the first day of school because it was hogging
the bathroom.

With the pig in the house, I was actually looking
FORWARD to school starting. But once I got
there I realized it was just the same old thing.

And, to be honest with you, I feel like I've been in middle school FOREVER.

I needed to mix things up a little or I was gonna go crazy. So in the first week of school I volunteered for the Homework Buddies programme.

But the main reason I signed up was so I could skip third period, which is Music class with Mrs Graziano.

To give you an idea of how long Mrs Graziano has been the music teacher, DAD had her when he was MY age. And apparently spending thirty years teaching middle-schoolers how to play musical instruments DOES something to a person.

Last week I met my Homework Buddy, this kid named Frew. I have no idea why he even signed up for the programme, though, because he's one of those people who reads scientific journals and college textbooks for FUN.

FREW

The first time we got together, Frew showed me his homework, which was some colouring and a word search. Frew said he didn't need any help, and then he asked to see MY homework.

I had at LEAST an hour of Maths problems and a Geography assignment that would've taken me ANOTHER two hours, but Frew whipped through all of it in about fifteen minutes.

SCRIBBLE
SCRIBBLE
SCRIBBLE

And he wasn't just fast, he was GOOD.
I turned in the assignments the next day, and when I got them back from my teachers I had perfect scores.

At first I felt a little bad about getting help
from a third-grader. But then I realized that
Homework Buddies are SUPPOSED to help each
other out.

So now whenever me and Frew get together I
just hand him a pile of assignments and let him do
his thing. The way I see it, this is working out
for everyone.

SCRIBBLE
SCRIBBLE
SCRIBBLE

My only complaint about Frew is that sometimes
he's TOO helpful. He's been getting bored
with my homework, so he started making up
assignments to CHALLENGE himself.

The other day he wrote a paper and attached it to my REGULAR homework for extra credit. But luckily I checked it over before handing it in.

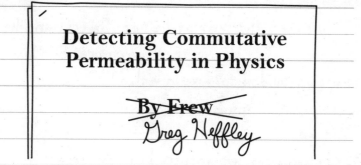

Detecting Commutative Permeability in Physics

~~By Frew~~
Greg Heffley

For a while I was just glad to be getting some homework help. But recently I've been thinking that, since I'm the one who "discovered" Frew, I deserve some kind of credit if he goes on to do big things.

<u>Wednesday</u>

As if our house wasn't crowded ENOUGH, now
GRANDPA is living with us.

They raised the rent at Leisure Towers, and he
couldn't afford to live there any more. So Mom
invited Grandpa to move in with OUR family.

Dad wasn't so hot on the idea, even though
Grandpa is his own father. But Mom says it will
be just like the old days, when three generations
lived under the same roof.

I think Mom has this rosy image of the way things
used to be, but I have a TOTALLY different
picture of what it must've been like back then.

I was actually OK with Grandpa moving in with us until I realized what it meant for ME. Mom let Grandpa pick any bedroom he wanted, and of course he chose MINE.

That meant I needed to find a new place to sleep. My first thought was to go to the guest room, but I forgot that's where the pig stays. And there's no WAY I'm sharing the sofa bed with a farm animal.

I ruled out RODRICK'S room right away, because he might actually be a step down from the PIG.

My only other choice was to room with MANNY, so I got out the air bed and set it up on his floor. But sleeping in Manny's room has its OWN problems.

Mom reads Manny a bedtime story every night, and sometimes they're really LONG. In fact, lately I think Manny's been picking out the thickest books he can find just to get on my nerves.

IN A HOLE IN THE GROUND THERE LIVED A HOBBIT.

Things have been a little tense ever since Grandpa moved in. You can tell he doesn't really approve of the way Mom and Dad are raising us kids, even though he never actually comes out and SAYS it.

Mom's been trying to potty train Manny FOREVER, and she's experimenting with something called "No Pants After Dinner".

And it's EXACTLY what it sounds like.

SKIP

What's SUPPOSED to happen is that when Manny feels the urge to GO he'll run to the bathroom.

But Manny just prances around all night with nothing on below the waist. And eventually he ducks behind the recliner in the family room.

I don't think Dad's a huge fan of No Pants After Dinner, but I can tell he's even MORE uncomfortable with Grandpa being here to witness it.

It's pretty obvious having Grandpa around is really stressing Dad out. And every time one of us kids screws up it just makes Dad even MORE tense.

What seems to annoy Dad the MOST is when
one of us kids asks Mom to do something that we
should be able to do OURSELVES.

Yesterday I asked Mom to open a microwave
burrito for me, because I always have trouble with
those plastic packages.

But Dad jumped all over my case. He said if I
was stranded on a desert island with a thousand
microwave burritos I'd STARVE to death
because I couldn't figure out how to open them
on my own.

I told Dad that the chances of me getting stranded on a desert island with a thousand microwave burritos were pretty slim, but he said I was missing the point.

He said if I don't learn how to do things by MYSELF I'm not gonna be able to survive in the "real world".

Another thing Dad hates is how Mom still helps me get ready for school in the morning. She picks out my clothes the night before, and she has a chart hanging in the kitchen to help me stay on track.

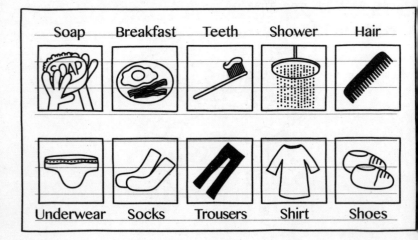

I guess Dad was pretty embarrassed by the chart, because the other day he took it down. But without that thing to guide me through the morning I got the order of things all wrong and ended up wearing socks over my shoes.

These days, I think Dad's just WAITING for me to screw up. This morning I forgot to put the cap back on the tube of toothpaste, and Dad was ready to POUNCE.

AHA!

I didn't think it was a big deal, but Dad gave me this long speech about how "little things have big consequences".

He said if I was a kid growing up in frontier times and it was my job to tighten the bolts on the wagon wheels but I FORGOT to, then the wheels would fall off and our family would get eaten by wolves.

I thought Dad was being kind of dramatic, but it DID make me feel a little guilty about that toothpaste cap.

I'm not the only one who's been getting on Dad's nerves, though. Lately, Rodrick's been getting under Dad's skin, too.

Whenever Rodrick needs petrol for his van, he asks Mom for money. But a few nights ago he made the mistake of doing it in front of Grandpa.

Dad said that from now on Rodrick has to pay for his OWN petrol. And, when Rodrick asked how he was supposed to do THAT, Dad said it was time for him to get a JOB.

So Mom helped Rodrick go through the Help
Wanted section of the newspaper to find him a
job that doesn't require any skills or experience.

They finally found an ad for a restaurant that's
about fifteen minutes from our house.

WANTED!

Seeking motivated individuals
to join the team at the

**OLD-TIMEY
ICE-CREAM
PARLOUR!**

Old-Timey Tobias

I went to the Old-Timey Ice-Cream Parlour
for Rowley's last birthday party, and that
experience may have PERMANENTLY ruined
ice cream for me.

They have this one dessert on the menu called the "Feeding Trough", which is FORTY scoops of ice cream all in one long tray. And when you mix different flavours of ice cream together it just turns into grey slop.

The Old-Timey Ice-Cream Parlour is one of those places where the whole staff comes to your table to sing for your birthday. That makes me really uncomfortable, because it's pretty obvious they'd rather be doing ANYTHING else.

Rodrick had an interview at the restaurant earlier in the week and, believe it or not, he got the job. Saturday was his first night of work, and Mom thought it would be a good idea for the rest of us to surprise Rodrick and cheer him on.

But when we got to the restaurant we couldn't find him anywhere. Mom was pretty worried, but eventually we found him out back.

Mom wasn't happy that Rodrick was on trash duty, and she gave the manager a piece of her mind.

But the manager said Rodrick was an "entry level" employee and that everyone who works at the restaurant has to pay their dues.

I'm pretty sure Rodrick was hoping we'd all just go home and leave him alone after that, but Mom wanted to stick around. And when Rodrick went on his fifteen-minute break we hung out with him in the employee lounge.

Rodrick spent the rest of the night taking the trash from the kitchen out to the dumpster, and I guess Mom wanted to see him one more time before we left. So she told our waiter it was Manny's birthday, and the waiter called the whole staff to our table.

But I wish Mom didn't go and do that, because there's something about the smell of garbage juice that really ruins your appetite.

...AND IF YOU'RE FEELIN' HUNGRY YOU'RE AT THE PERFECT PLACE NOW JUST BLOW OUT THAT CANDLE SO YOU CAN STUFF YER FACE!

Monday

Lately, Mom's been trying to get Grandpa to tell us kids about what life was like when HE was growing up.

Grandpa says that when he was young they didn't have televisions or anything like that, so kids spent most of their time outdoors playing games like Kick the Can.

Grown-ups are ALWAYS talking about playing Kick the Can. One time me and Rowley actually gave it a try to see what the big deal was, but we quit after about thirty seconds.

Dad says when he was a kid he and his best friend, Giles, would just use their imaginations and play all day in the woods.

Well, me and Rowley tried using OUR imaginations once, but Rowley's dad put an end to it before we could even get going.

ROWLEY JEFFERSON! YOU PUT DOWN THAT STICK RIGHT THIS INSTANT!

Dad said today's parents are overprotective and that when he was a kid he and Giles roamed free and never even bothered to tell their parents where they were going.

But Mom said it was a lot SAFER back in those days, and now it's too dangerous for kids to be off on their own without adult supervision. Dad said that might be true, but kids like me and Rowley need to learn how to PROTECT ourselves.

Dad said when he was in middle school he and Giles buried stuff all over town so that if they ever got cornered they could fight their way out.

But Grandpa had a different version of things. He said Dad and Giles raided the kitchen drawer for silverware, and THAT'S what they stashed all over the neighbourhood.

When Dad's mother realized her forks and knives were missing she made the boys dig them all up and bring them BACK.

After that, Dad and Giles got their hands on some PLASTIC utensils. But they got into an argument over whether or not a spork could be used for self-defence, and things turned ugly.

Giles told his mother what Dad did and showed her the spork marks to prove it. I guess those must've been different times, because Giles's mom bent Dad over her knee and SPANKED him.

See, that's the problem with putting too much stock in the old days. You remember all the GOOD stuff, but you forget about the time you got spanked by your best friend's mom.

Wednesday
I guess I thought Grandpa would live with us for a little while and then find a place that was cheaper than Leisure Towers. But now I'm starting to worry that it's PERMANENT.

And that's not a good thing, because I'm not sure how much longer I can be Manny's roommate.

For one thing, it's not dignified to share a room with a person who doesn't wear pants after dinner.

And Grandpa's almost just as bad. When he moved out of Leisure Towers, his girlfriend, Darlene, broke up with him. Lately, he's been moping around the house in a bathrobe, which means I can't really have friends over.

I figure the sooner Grandpa's back in the game, the sooner he moves out. So I've been showing Grandpa how to do online dating to help him break out of his funk.

I think I've created a MONSTER, though. Now Grandpa's on the computer twenty-four hours a day, and he's got at LEAST fifty relationships going simultaneously.

Don't even ask me how he keeps track of who's who.

Belinda has sent you a wink

Bethany would like to meet you

Martha likes your profile picture

Tiffany has sent you a poke

Sylvie likes your knock-knock joke

Marjorie thinks you are nice

Things are starting to turn around for Rodrick, too. He told Mom he got a promotion at work, so of course tonight we had to pile into the car to go and show him our support.

I'm not sure if I'd call Rodrick's new position a PROMOTION, though. They've got him dressing up as Old-Timey Tobias, the restaurant's mascot.

Apparently the guy who had the job LAST got fired for being seen without his head on. And I'm guessing when it comes to mascots that's a HUGE no-no.

Old-Timey Tobias is supposed to walk around the restaurant and go from table to table making little kids happy. But, as far as I can tell, he has the OPPOSITE effect.

In fact, kids seem to really HATE Old-Timey Tobias. When we got there tonight, Rodrick was getting it from every side.

Rodrick told Mom that his manager warned him if he was ever caught without his Tobias head on he'd be fired on the spot.

Luckily, one of the eyes on the costume's head comes out, which is the only way Rodrick is able to stay hydrated.

I'm starting to wonder if the guy who had the job dressing up as Old-Timey Tobias got fired on PURPOSE.

If I had to bet on how long Rodrick lasts, I'd give him two weeks, tops.

<u>Friday</u>
All the buzz at school has been about this big trip to Hardscrabble Farms that's coming up next month.

When you get to my grade, the whole class goes on a week-long trip to this place where you sleep in log cabins and learn about nature and hard work.

I'm sure it's a blast if you're into that sort of thing, but I've already decided I'm gonna be the one kid who stays BACK when everybody else heads off on the trip.

And while the REST of my classmates are sweating it out in the woods I'll be in the school library enjoying all the comforts of the modern world.

Mom's been trying to get me to change my mind because she thinks I'll regret not going.

I really doubt that's gonna happen, though. I've heard horror stories from kids who went away to Hardscrabble Farms, and I remember the letters Rodrick sent home when HE went there.

In fact, Rodrick seemed kind of traumatized by the whole experience. When he got back from the trip he crawled into bed and stayed there for an entire weekend.

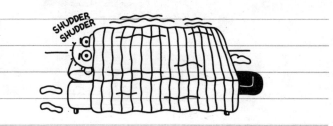

Today was the deadline for picking who you wanted to room with, and at lunch everyone was scrambling to get into a good cabin. I was glad I'd already decided I wasn't going, because I really didn't want to deal with all that drama.

I felt a little bad for Rowley because he was counting on bunking with ME. When I told him I wasn't going on the trip, he went around seeing if anyone had an opening in their cabin.

47

But by the end of the lunch period things weren't looking good for him.

I can't really worry about Rowley, though, because I've got my OWN problems to deal with.

Monday, Mom and Dad got a letter from the school saying they had to come in for a special parent-teacher conference.

I've been worried sick all week because I thought I must've forgotten to cross off Frew's name on one of my homework assignments and I was in trouble.

But that wasn't it at ALL.

The reason the school asked Mom and Dad to come in was to tell them my homework grades have improved so much that they're putting me in harder classes.

Well, I'm sure Frew will appreciate having more challenging homework, but he can't be there to help me during TESTS. So, unless I can figure out a way to sneak him into school, I'm never gonna pass.

When Mom and Dad came home from the parent-teacher conference, Mom said we needed to celebrate the "good news".

Of course THAT meant going to the Old-Timey Ice-Cream Parlour.

I was getting a little sick of spending every night at Rodrick's work, and I think Grandpa was feeling the same way. He told Mom ice cream makes his gums hurt and he was gonna stay home this time around.

I tried using the same excuse, but Mom was dead set on us going.

When we got to the restaurant, though, Rodrick was nowhere to be found. The manager told Mom that Rodrick never showed up for work.

That sent Mom into a PANIC, and we got back in the van to go and look for him. We drove all over the place, and we finally found Rodrick walking along the side of the highway.

TRUDGE
TRUDGE

When we pulled over, Rodrick got in the van and explained what happened. He said there was a traffic jam on the highway and he was gonna be late for work. So he got into the car-pool lane, where he could go a lot FASTER.

But the rule for the car-pool lane is that you have to have at least TWO people in your vehicle.

So Rodrick made it look like Old-Timey Tobias was sitting next to him in the passenger seat.

Unfortunately, some eagle-eyed cop pulled him over.

The cop wasn't amused and gave Rodrick a ticket for one hundred dollars. Then he found all sorts of things wrong with the van, like a broken tail light and an expired inspection sticker.

After that, the cop had Rodrick's van towed and left him stranded on the side of the road. So Rodrick was a HUGE target for all the kids who were stuck in the traffic jam.

Mom told Dad to drive home so she could throw Rodrick's costume in the washing machine. But when we got to our street there were cars parked up and down on both sides.

There were even cars parked on our LAWN, which was pretty strange.

We had to park the van at the bottom of the hill and walk up the street. When we finally got to our yard, you could hear loud music coming from the house.

And when we opened the front door there was a RAGING party going on inside.

We had to push through the crowd to find Grandpa, who was out back in our old hot tub. And, from the look of things, he was having the time of his LIFE.

Dad kicked everyone out of the house, which took FOREVER, mostly because no one was in a big hurry to leave.

When everyone was gone, Dad lit into Grandpa for having a party.

Grandpa said he didn't PLAN on having a party. He said he tried to invite ONE lady from his dating site over to watch a movie, but he must've accidentally hit "send all". And then everyone showed up at once.

Dad was really mad, but it must've been awkward for him to come up with a punishment for his own father.

I guess he couldn't think of anything better, so he just put Grandpa in the time-out corner.

I wish we had done a better job of clearing out the party guests when we got home, though, because there were a few stragglers in Manny's room who didn't poke their heads out until they thought the coast was clear.

Tuesday
Ever since Grandpa had his party, Dad hasn't been willing to leave him home alone. And when DAD can't be there to watch him he makes one of US do it.

Grandpa's supposed to sit in time-out for an hour a day to work off his punishment, but he likes to do that in front of the television instead of in the corner.

So if you're on Grandpa duty you have to watch whatever HE wants to watch.

But during the school day Grandpa is home ALONE, and I think Dad's nervous there's gonna be another party.

So he went out and bought one of those webcams to make sure there isn't any funny business going on while he's at work.

I don't know where he PUT it, exactly. But what I DO know is that he's not just using it to keep an eye on GRANDPA.

I'm all for technology, but not when it's used AGAINST me. I don't like having a camera in the house, because nowadays there are cameras everywhere you turn.

And if you ever do something embarrassing in a public place, trust me, it's gonna get recorded.

But the worst thing is camera phones, because nowadays EVERYBODY'S got one.

59

Last summer when I was getting out of the town pool, my bathing suit fell down a little and everyone saw it happen.

And, before I even dried off, the pictures were posted all over the Internet.

These days you can even get in trouble for taking a picture of YOURSELF. A few months ago we went to brunch after church, and when we left the restaurant I felt like I might have spinach in my teeth.

I wasn't anywhere near a mirror, so I borrowed Mom's phone to take a picture of myself, just to make sure.

But some lady in front of me thought I was taking a photo of HER, and she wouldn't let us leave until she looked through the pictures on Mom's phone to make sure I HADN'T.

Now that I think of it, that might've been what started Mom on this electronics-free idea to begin with.

Speaking of which, Mom got all the signatures she needed to take her petition to the town hall.

The way she GOT them was by intercepting all the partygoers as they were leaving our house the other night.

After Mom took the petition to the town hall, the leaders had a vote and made it official. So this Saturday the whole town is going to voluntarily unplug for the weekend.

Mom's made it her mission to get the word out to as many people as possible. I'm trying to keep a low profile until this whole thing is over, but Mom hasn't been making it easy.

I think cutting ourselves off from the outside world is a bad idea. If there's a zombie apocalypse or something big like that, we're gonna be the LAST ones to know.

<u>Friday</u>

As part of this electronics-free weekend, everyone's supposed to come down to the town park tomorrow for a voluntary clean-up.

But it's gonna take a lot more than one afternoon to make a dent in THAT mess.

These days, the park looks like something out of a movie where there's been a nuclear war.

The park used to be NICE, but things went downhill when the town ran out of money.

The main reason was because they voted to build a one-way "mobile phone only" path through the park, since half the time people on the REGULAR path weren't watching where they were going.

So all the money that was supposed to go towards regular clean-up went to this new path for people who wanted to use their electronic devices while they walked.

But the project got too expensive, and they had to cancel it before they finished the footbridge over the creek.

The park got really run-down after that, and families stopped coming once teenagers took over. So, if the people organizing this clean-up are smart, the first thing they'll do is find an exterminator that specializes in teenagers.

Saturday
I have no idea what time I woke up this morning because the clock on Manny's dresser was unplugged. In fact, EVERYTHING in the house was unplugged, which goes to show that Mom was taking this electronics-free thing pretty literally.

The next thing I noticed was that there were a
LOT of people out walking in the neighbourhood.
So I guess everyone had decided to get into the
"old-time" spirit.

I was planning on just relaxing and reading
comic books on the couch all day, but Dad said I
should take advantage of all the "foot traffic".

He said when HE was a kid he and Giles opened a
lemonade stand and earned enough money to buy
them each a new skateboard. I said I thought a
lemonade stand was a GREAT idea.

Dad surprised me by handing over twenty dollars in "seed money" to help me get started.

I knew I was gonna need a business partner, so I called Rowley and told him to come down.

I figured we'd get going by looking up the recipe for lemonade on the Internet, but Mom had hidden the power cord to the computer. I was a little embarrassed to ask Dad, so me and Rowley decided to wing it.

I knew we'd need lemons for sure, so we rode our bikes down to the convenience store and bought out their whole supply.

When we got back home, we didn't know the exact number of lemons to put in the pitcher. So we went on the high side just to be safe.

I was pretty sure the only other ingredient for lemonade besides water is SUGAR, but we didn't know how much of THAT we were supposed to use, either. So we just eyeballed it.

I thought after that we were pretty much good to go, but then Dad came downstairs, saw what we were doing and told us we got it all wrong.

Dad said that, first of all, the GREEN lemons we bought were actually LIMES, so we had to get rid of those.

Then he said that to make lemonade we needed to cut the lemons in HALF and SQUEEZE them into the water. Which would've been nice to know at the beginning.

But Rowley was too scared to cut the lemons because he said they'd make his eyes water. I told him he was getting lemons confused with ONIONS.

He wasn't budging, though, and I knew I had to do something about it or he wouldn't help out.

So I dug around in the garage until I found a mask Rowley could cover his eyes with.

Once Rowley calmed down, we started cutting the lemons, which was a LOT harder than I thought it would be.

When I sliced into the FIRST lemon, I got a shot of juice right in my eye.

It stung like CRAZY, and I could barely see. Rowley took the snorkel out of his mouth and started in with the whole "I told you so" stuff, but I didn't wanna hear it.

After I got my vision back, we squeezed all of our lemons into the water and set up our stand on the pavement.

A few people stopped by, but it was just to criticize everything we were doing. One lady told us we needed to stir the lemonade to mix the sugar in better. But even after we did THAT she wouldn't make a purchase.

Another guy who tasted our lemonade complained that it was too SWEET.

The next few people said the same thing. So I dumped out half the pitcher and added more water. But people didn't like where I GOT it from.

One guy had a problem with the fact that we were using the same glass for every customer, even though I explained to him that we were rinsing it out after every use.

We got tired of sitting out in the hot sun and decided our lemonade stand would work just as well as a self-serve business. So we put out a jar where people could pay for what they drank.

But the second you set up an honour system somebody's gotta go and ruin it for EVERYONE.

We realized we were just gonna have to suck it up and man the lemonade stand full-time. So we got another glass from the kitchen cabinet and headed back outside.

I started to notice that the people walking UP the hill looked a lot thirstier than the people walking DOWN it. So we posted a new pricing policy to take full advantage.

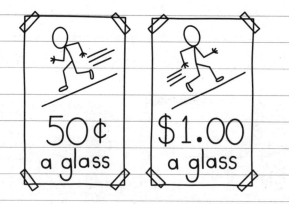

A couple of people thought our jar was for TIPS, and they dropped in some loose change. After that, we started pushing the tips, because any money we brought in that way was 100% profit.

I was starting to feel good about things until a kid named Cedric Cunningham set up his OWN lemonade stand a few houses down.

And it was pretty obvious he had help from his parents, because HIS stand made ours look like a JOKE.

See, this is the problem when you have an original idea. Five seconds later you've got a million copycats.

I'm a professional, though, and I wasn't gonna take a little competition personally. So I offered Cedric two bucks to take his lemonade stand down, and he agreed to it.

But a minute later he set up his stand again, this time directly across the street from us.

I was getting pretty annoyed because we were running out of lemonade and I knew Dad wasn't gonna give us any more money for ingredients.

That's when I realized if we sold WATER instead of lemonade we would save ourselves a lot of hassle.

Plus, it was pretty obvious Cedric had cornered the lemonade market, ESPECIALLY after he put up his new sign.

But I knew if we were gonna sell water it would have to seem extra-special to get people to PAY for it. So I came up with an awesome-sounding name, and then I filled Manny's baby pool with water so we wouldn't run out for a while.

If we were gonna call this stuff "fitness water", we'd have to let people know it actually WORKED. So I had Rowley do some jumping jacks and push-ups in front of our stand.

The problem is Rowley's not in the best shape, so it was a bad look for our company.

Luckily, a guy who was actually in shape came up the hill right after that, and I offered to pay him a few bucks if he told everyone he got that way by drinking our NRG Fitness Water.

But I guess he had better things to do, because he told us he wasn't interested.

Unfortunately, a guy walking DOWN the hill overheard us, and he said he'd be HAPPY to endorse our product.

Not to be mean or anything but this guy definitely did not have the look we were after.

So, to make him go away, I paid him three bucks to tell people he DIDN'T drink our stuff.

I realized we were still competing for beverage dollars with the kid across the street and that if we were gonna make any REAL money we needed to move our operation to a whole new market.

And I knew just the place: the town park.

With the big clean-up going on down there,
I figured there would be a TON of thirsty
volunteers. So me and Rowley loaded up a wagon
with as much of our product as we could carry
and headed down the hill.

Halfway to the park, Rowley said he was dehydrated
and needed a drink. I didn't wanna stop, but he
looked like he was gonna pass out. So I let him
take a bottle and made a note to dock his pay
later on.

When we got down to the park, it seemed like the whole TOWN was there. Everyone was working really hard, and it was pretty hot out.

As a BONUS, the water fountain was broken, which meant people didn't have any real options for quenching their thirst. So me and Rowley knew we were gonna make a KILLING selling our stuff.

Unfortunately, Mom spotted us right away and asked what we were up to.

I told her we were gonna sell our fitness water to anyone who was willing to shell out a few bucks.

But Mom said it was "tacky" to profit off a bunch of volunteers who were sacrificing their Saturday to clean up the park. I told her everybody who drank our water would be able to volunteer TWICE as hard, and the whole clean-up would go a lot quicker.

While me and Mom were arguing about this, the ladies who were working on the flower bed totally raided our supplies.

And, before we could do anything about it, they had poured our whole inventory of fitness water into the ground like it was just some cheap junk.

I did a quick calculation and figured that was at least two hundred dollars in lost profits seeping into the ground. But those ladies just went right back to their planting like it was no big deal.

Still, it wasn't too late for me and Rowley to turn this thing around. We gathered up the empty bottles and headed down to the creek for a refill.

Mom stepped in our way. She told me and Rowley she wanted us to help the volunteers with the clean-up and handed us some gardening tools to get started.

I explained that we were BUSINESSMEN and REAL businessmen don't work for free. But, before I was even done talking, Rowley was on his hands and knees planting perennials.

I knew I had to get out of there as quickly as possible or I'D get roped in, too. But Mom was one step ahead of me.

She said when I was little she used to take me to the park every day, and that those were her most special memories of the two of us.

She told me if we DIDN'T clean the park OTHER moms wouldn't be able to have the same kinds of precious moments with THEIR kids.

See, Mom knows EXACTLY how to get to me. And that's the reason I found myself raking leaves for FREE instead of making a truckload of money.

The rake Mom gave me was a piece of junk, though, but when I asked for a new one she said everybody was doing their best with what they had.

It took me half an hour to scrape together a measly pile of leaves, and then a bunch of little kids came tearing through it and undid all my hard work.

WHEEEEEEEE!

Don't ask me why people brought their little kids to the park clean-up, because they were no help at ALL. In fact, they were CONSTANTLY getting into trouble.

At one point a bunch of them were playing in a pile of fertilizer, and someone had to chase them out of there.

The whole park clean-up effort was TOTALLY disorganized. Nobody was really in charge, so it was just complete CHAOS.

Things got even CRAZIER when a bus pulled into the parking lot and a bunch of teenagers in orange jumpsuits filed out.

Apparently these guys were bussed in to serve
their punishment for committing crimes like
shoplifting and vandalism. And, if I had to guess,
I'd say a few of them were directly responsible for
the graffiti on the playground equipment.

The community-service guys were more interested
in goofing off than pitching in. And some
of the stuff they were doing was downright
DANGEROUS.

But, right when it seemed like it couldn't get any
worse, a bunch of vans rolled into the parking
lot and an entire Girl Scout troop poured out of
the vehicles.

And it looked like they meant BUSINESS.

Within ten minutes, they had organized everyone at the park clean-up into separate teams, with a Girl Scout in charge of each one.

My team was responsible for raking leaves in the playground area, and the girl in charge of my group was a Brownie.

It was a little embarrassing, but, to be honest with you, I was HAPPY the Girl Scouts came in and whipped everybody into shape.

Every time I've seen the Girl Scouts get involved with a project, I've been IMPRESSED.

A few months ago, the town wanted to build a community garden, but nobody could get their act together and the project fizzled out.

But then the Girl Scouts swooped in and built the whole thing on a Sunday afternoon.

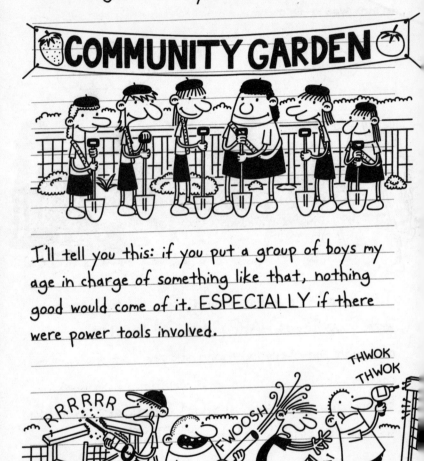

COMMUNITY GARDEN

I'll tell you this: if you put a group of boys my age in charge of something like that, nothing good would come of it. ESPECIALLY if there were power tools involved.

RRRRRR

FWOOSH

THWOK
THWOK

Even though they were at the town park to work, the Girl Scouts weren't gonna let an opportunity to do some fundraising pass them by. They set up a stand to sell cookies, and one of their first customers was MOM. So I guess she'd changed her mind about people selling stuff to volunteers.

I was glad the Girl Scouts were running the show, but they were working us HARD. After an hour of raking, I was worn out and wanted to go home. But it was clear they weren't letting ANYONE go until the last leaf was bagged.

Another person in my group who seemed a little worn out was my Homework Buddy, Frew.

OTHER people figured out how smart Frew is, and a bunch of grown-ups started bugging him for stuff they'd usually get from their PHONES.

I noticed that every half hour the Girl Scouts rotated from group to group. So, during a changing of the guard, I saw my opportunity and TOOK it.

I knew EXACTLY where I was headed, too: the creek.

When I was on the swim team in first grade, Dad used to drop me off at the town pool every day. But the MINUTE he drove away I'd run down to the creek and catch minnows until practice was over.

I'd always make sure I got back to the pool before Dad came to pick me up, and I'd jump in at the last second so it looked like I'd been swimming the whole time.

HOP

But, once, Dad came EARLY to watch me practise, and I guess I got carried away catching minnows.

So I ended up getting to the pool AFTER Dad and I got busted.

Today, I figured I'd just take a quick breather down by the creek and then get back to work.

But thirty seconds after I got there I heard somebody crashing through the bushes.

It turns out Frew had seen me take off from the playground, and he FOLLOWED me.

Frew said he couldn't handle all the pestering from the grown-ups a second longer, and when he saw me leave he thought I had the right idea.

While we were talking, we heard something BIG coming our way. I thought it might be a BEAR, but I was pretty shocked to see that it was one of the community-service guys.

In fact, I KNEW this guy. His name was Billy Rotner, and he used to hang out in our basement when Rodrick's band practised.

A month or so ago, I heard Rodrick telling one of his friends that Billy got caught stealing a pack of sour gummy worms at the convenience store.

I really wasn't happy this guy had followed me to my hiding spot. I told Billy he should go back to the park before he got us ALL in trouble.

But Billy said he was making a run for it and was NEVER going back to community service.

Then Billy started blubbering about how when he was little his mom bought a pack of sour gummy worms for him and his brother to share, but his brother wouldn't give him a single worm and ate the whole pack.

CHEW CHEW

Billy said the only reason he stole from the convenience store was so he could finally have a pack of sour gummy worms all to HIMSELF.

I was getting really uncomfortable listening to this guy go on and on, and I was hoping Frew would help me talk some sense into him.

But then Frew started with a speech of his OWN.

Frew started talking about how his parents make him get up at 5:00 in the morning six days a week to study for the geography bee, and how he's never got to play laser tag because his parents say it's a waste of time.

This was all getting to be a little much for me, and I decided I'd rather be raking leaves than listening to these guys tell their sob stories.

So I started heading back to the playground.
But all of a sudden that Brownie appeared out of
nowhere and TOTALLY caught me off guard.

My instincts kicked in and I RAN. Frew and
Billy saw me take off, and they were right on
my heels.

But the Brownie was carrying a WHISTLE and,
the next thing I knew, the whole Girl Scout
troop was in hot pursuit.

I started to run FASTER when I realized
me and Frew might get in serious trouble for
harbouring a fugitive.

I didn't know if the Girl Scouts actually had the authority to ARREST anyone, but I wasn't gonna stick around to find out.

For all I knew, that was something they needed to do to earn one of their badges.

Once the chase was on, Billy took the lead, and me and Frew just followed HIM. It was pretty obvious he'd had experience with this kind of thing, because he seemed to know what he was doing.

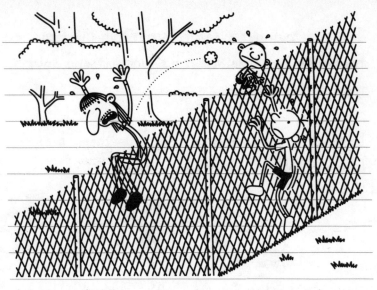

After a while, we were able to put some distance
between ourselves and the Girl Scouts, and we
could barely hear the whistle. So we stopped for
a minute to catch our breath.

Billy said we were gonna need our energy to stay
ahead of the Girl Scouts.

Then he took out a few rolls of Thin Mint cookies that were tucked away in his jumpsuit and split them up between us.

I'm just gonna assume he PAID for them, because if he HADN'T I don't wanna know.

After we fuelled up on cookies, Billy said we should all ditch our CLOTHES, because if they used DOGS to track us we could throw them off our trail.

Then it dawned on me that if this guy couldn't get away with stealing a pack of sour gummy worms he was probably the LAST person I should be taking this kind of advice from.

I realized I'd made a HUGE mistake and started looking for a way out of the situation. So I told the guys we should split up, saying if we DID we'd be harder to catch.

But Frew said we should stick TOGETHER.

He said we could travel around the country and have crazy adventures, and maybe even join the circus somewhere along the way.

Billy seemed to like that idea, too. Then the two of them started arguing over who should get the money for the movie rights to our story if we ever became famous.

I decided to use the opportunity to try and slip away. But, when I turned to leave, a group of vans appeared out of NOWHERE.

RUMBLE   RUMBLE

Mom was in the lead van, and the Girl Scouts were in the vehicles right behind her.

There was a second there when I thought Frew might try to make a last-ditch attempt to escape.

But after all his big talk about life on the run he totally fell to pieces.

I thought Mom would be really mad, but she seemed RELIEVED. She wanted to know what I was thinking, running away like that.

I figured Billy was going down no matter WHAT. And there was no use in all THREE of us getting in trouble. So I pinned the whole thing on HIM.

I guess I feel a little bad. But, to be fair, stealing the Thin Mints was HIS idea.

I don't know how much community service they're gonna tack on to Billy's sentence. But by the time he's DONE I plan to be attending a university halfway across the country.

The craziest thing of all was the way Mom found us in the FIRST place.

When she got that GPS chip for the PIG, she got one for ME, too. So I've been walking around with one of those things attached to my shoelace for the past two months without even knowing it.

And when I disappeared from the park Mom used her PHONE to figure out where I was.

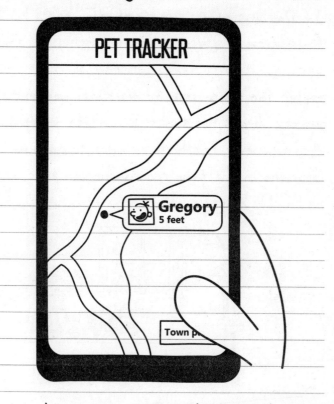

Now's not the time to complain about Mom being overprotective, though. Because if she hadn't come to my rescue I might've ended up in a travelling circus with Frew and Billy.

But, still, so much for Mom going "electronics-free".

<u>Friday</u>

If Dad was on my case BEFORE, he's a hundred times worse NOW.

After the town-park incident last weekend, it's pretty obvious he thinks I can't be trusted. And whenever he's home he likes to have me and Grandpa in the same room so he can keep an eye on BOTH of us.

I wish I never knew about the webcam, though, because it's got me really paranoid. There could actually be MULTIPLE cameras in the house.

I'm pretty sure there's one in Manny's stuffed duck, because its eyes seem to follow me.

If there's NOT a camera in there, then I've been making a pretty big fool out of myself the past few days.

Luckily, Mom took Dad to the airport to go on a business trip this morning, and I know he can't monitor me the whole time he's away. Still, I've been extra careful not to screw up, just in case he's got one of those webcams recording to a hard drive somewhere.

This morning when I was brushing my teeth I made sure to put the toothpaste cap back on the tube the way Dad always tells me.

But my fingers were slippery, and I dropped the cap in the sink.

It bounced around a few times, then it went
right down the drain.

I knew that the SECOND Dad got home from
his trip he'd go to the upstairs bathroom to make
sure the cap was on the toothpaste. So I had to
get it BACK.

The first thing I did was try and fish the cap
out of the drain with a cotton bud. But all I
managed to pull up was a bunch of hair and
other gunk.

And now that I know what's in people's sinks I guarantee you I'll never be a plumber.

I figured I'd probably pushed the toothpaste cap even FURTHER down the drain with that cotton bud, so I opened the cabinet under the sink to see if I could figure out where it ended up.

I knew Dad had a bunch of do-it-yourself books on plumbing in the basement, and I figured there'd be some step-by-step instructions that showed exactly how to fix this sort of thing.

I couldn't make heads nor tails of the diagrams in the book, so I took my best shot at it. There was a plastic tube underneath the sink, and I figured the toothpaste cap must be somewhere inside.

So I loosened the nut that held the tube to the metal pipe, and the tube came out pretty easily.

I guess I was supposed to turn off a valve or something, though, because the next thing I knew water was spraying out all over the place.

It took me a minute to figure out how to shut off the valve, and by the time I did there was a huge puddle on the floor.

I soaked up as much water as I could with the towels that were in the bathroom. Then I ran down the stairs to get some more out of the laundry room.

But when I got down to the kitchen I realized I had a BIGGER problem.

I told Grandpa where the water was coming from, but he didn't seem too concerned. He said the only REAL damage would be a water stain on the kitchen ceiling.

I'm glad Grandpa thought it was no big deal, but I'm sure Dad would see the situation DIFFERENTLY.

I begged Grandpa to help me out of this mess, and he told me he would. Grandpa said there's a special kind of paint that covers up water stains, and he'd take me to the hardware store to get it.

That sounded GREAT. He grabbed Dad's keys and we got in the car. But when we backed out of the driveway Grandpa clipped a trash can.

I wasn't too concerned, but when we hit a neighbour's MAILBOX I started to get worried.

I realized I couldn't remember the last time I was in a car with Grandpa at the wheel. And all of a sudden it hit me: last year, Grandpa failed his driver's test, so they took away his LICENCE.

He hasn't been allowed to drive since.

I was really nervous, so I told Grandpa maybe we should go back home. But now that he was on the open road there was no turning back.

By the time we got out of our neighbourhood, he seemed to be getting the hang of it. But I was still pretty worried when we got on the ramp for the highway.

Luckily, there weren't a lot of people driving at that time of day, and the hardware store was only a few miles away.

The weird thing was all of the signs along the side of the road were facing the wrong way, which was really confusing.

When I saw two cars coming towards us, I realized that somehow Grandpa had taken the EXIT ramp instead of the ENTRANCE ramp, and we were headed in the WRONG DIRECTION.

Grandpa slammed on the brakes, and the car did a 180 before coming to a stop in the breakdown lane. It's a MIRACLE we didn't get hit, and our near-death experience really shook both of us up.

Suddenly a water stain on the kitchen ceiling didn't seem like such a big deal any more. Me and Grandpa agreed we should just go back home and call it a day.

At least NOW we were headed in the right direction. But when Grandpa put the car in drive it rolled a few feet, then conked out.

SPUTTER
SPUTTER

At first I thought something must've happened to the car when Grandpa slammed on the brakes, but when I looked at the dashboard I realized we were out of PETROL.

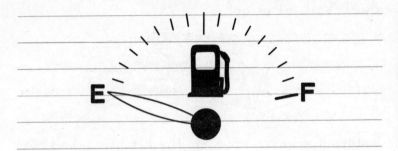

Rodrick used the car last night when he went to work, and of COURSE he didn't refuel it.

Grandpa saw a sign ahead that said there was a service station a mile up the road, and he told me he was gonna walk there and bring back a can of petrol so we could get home.

I wanted to go WITH him, but he said I should stay in the car so it didn't get towed by the highway department. I didn't feel great about the whole idea, but I figured it was the only choice I had.

Grandpa headed off on foot, and I waited for what must've been an HOUR. I was starting to get a little worried, and then I looked up at the rear-view mirror and saw something in the distance.

A group of people were walking towards the car along the side of the road. At first I was excited, because I thought they might be able to HELP. But when I saw their orange jumpsuits I FROZE.

It was the community-service gang, and they were coming my way.

When they got closer, I saw that one of them was that guy BILLY. I thought about making a run for it, but I didn't want to take my chances out in the open.

I did the only other thing I could think of,
which was to lock the doors and HIDE. There
aren't a whole lot of good hiding places in a CAR,
though, so the best I could do was get down
underneath the dashboard and stay really still.

Then I held my breath and prayed. It took
FOREVER for those guys to get to the car,
and when they finally DID they decided it was a
good place to take their lunch break.

SLURP

MUNCH

CHEW
CHEW

Eventually the community-service crew finished eating and moved on. But they left a huge mess, which just goes to show they weren't taking their highway clean-up duties too seriously.

Once I was sure they were gone, I got back up. But BOTH of my legs had fallen asleep from being in such an awkward position for that long, so I grabbed the handle on the centre console to pull myself up.

But the handle MOVED and, when it did, so did the CAR.

I had accidentally shifted the car into NEUTRAL, and it started to roll FORWARD.

The car was picking up speed, so I stepped on the brake. But it locked up, and the car just kept going. I was afraid I was gonna roll out into traffic and get hit.

Then I saw GRANDPA walking towards me in the breakdown lane, and I PANICKED.

I jerked the steering wheel left and just BARELY missed Grandpa. The problem was the car rolled right into a DITCH. And that's where it stayed until Mom came two hours later with the towing company.

If I had to do it all over again, I would've just left that toothpaste cap in the drain.

Monday
I BEGGED Mom not to tell Dad what happened to the car when he got home.

But she said since the bumper was all banged up he'd find out ANYWAY.

I realized my only option was to get out of town. And I thought of the PERFECT way to do it.

The class trip to Hardscrabble Farms starts today and goes for a whole WEEK. I figure by the time I get BACK Dad will have cooled down, at least a little.

So I told Mom I changed my mind about the trip, and she was all excited.

She called the school to make sure I could still go, and luckily there were a handful of spaces left in the cabins.

I went through my book bag and found the packing list they sent home last month to check what I needed to bring.

Hardscrabble Farms Supply List

Bug spray   Jeans
Hiking boots   Plastic bag
Raincoat   Sunscreen
Flask   Toiletries
Backpack   Wool socks

NO electronic devices
NO junk food

It was too late to go out and shop for all that stuff. Luckily, Mom found Rodrick's duffel bag in the garage, which he had never unpacked from when HE went on the trip a few years ago.

Inside were some hiking boots, a raincoat, a flask, bug spray and a bunch of other things on the list, which was great.

But the bag REEKED because there was a half-eaten ham sandwich in there, which had something growing out of it.

I was a little worried about the food situation at camp, and I was tempted to try and sneak a few candy bars in. But I wasn't sure what the penalty was if you got CAUGHT, so I decided to just hide them in my sock drawer so nobody would eat them while I was gone.

I wasn't willing to take any risks when it came to my COMFORT, though.

I stuffed three whole containers of Freshies into Rodrick's bag, even though that meant I couldn't fit the raincoat.

I buried the Freshies at the bottom of the bag because I didn't want Mom to know I was taking them. Mom says baby wipes are too expensive for everyone to use on a regular basis and they're reserved for MANNY.

See, this is the main reason I want to be rich when I'm older. When I have a ton of money, I can buy as many baby wipes as I WANT.

But until I have money of my own I'll have to keep raiding Manny's supply.

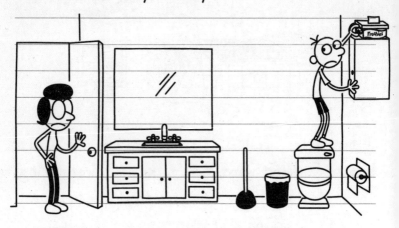

When I was just about ready to leave for the trip, Grandpa gave me a book he said might come in handy.

Grandpa said the book belonged to him as a kid, and he gave it to Dad when HE was my age. Now he wanted ME to have it.

It looked a little outdated to me, but I didn't want to hurt Grandpa's feelings. So I told him I'd take it with me and read it the first chance I got.

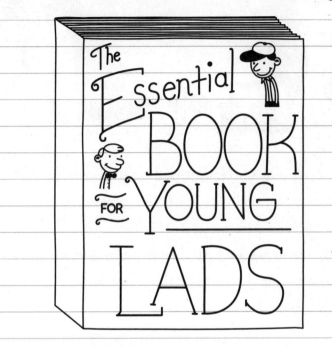

There was JUST enough room to fit it in my bag, and I figured the more stuff piled on top of the Freshies, the better.

When Mom dropped me off at school this morning, though, I realized I was SERIOUSLY unprepared for this trip.

Everybody else had a TON of gear, and I felt like I had underpacked.

After all our stuff was loaded onto the bus, the bags took up at least half the space.

That meant we had to double up on seats, which made the ride to Hardscrabble Farms feel a LOT longer than it should've.

When we finally got there and drove through the main entrance, I was pretty relieved. But the last stretch was BRUTAL because it was a dirt road.

When we got off the bus, a group of kids from another school was just leaving. And they looked like they couldn't be getting out of there soon enough.

A kid in the back was holding a handwritten sign that didn't make any sense to me.

A couple of my classmates seemed pretty freaked out when they saw it. A boy standing next to me said his older brother went to Hardscrabble Farms a few years back and told him all about Silas Scratch.

Apparently this Silas Scratch guy was a farmer who lived at Hardscrabble Farms a long time ago, but then the county came in and kicked him off his land.

Another kid chimed in and said HE heard Silas Scratch went to live in the forest, where he survived by eating slugs and berries. Then Melinda Henson said she heard he went CRAZY and grew his fingernails really long.

See, I could've done without the part about the long fingernails, because that sort of thing really gives me the willies.

One of our chaperones, Mr Healey, said that when HIS class went to Hardscrabble Farms a kid named Frankie came across Silas Scratch's shack in the woods. And after Frankie saw it he was never the same.

Anyone who hadn't heard of Silas Scratch BEFORE knew about him NOW, because the story spread like wildfire.

I found the whole Silas Scratch thing disturbing.

I GUARANTEE you, if anyone told me there was a deranged farmer prowling the grounds of Hardscrabble Farms, I would've just stayed home and taken my chances with DAD.

After we were done unloading the bus, we brought our stuff down to the main lodge, which was a giant log cabin with a bunch of long tables inside.

The person in charge was Mrs Graziano, and once everyone sat down she gave a speech about the camp rules. There were a BUNCH of them, but the one she said was most important was that boys and girls aren't allowed to visit each other's cabins for any reason.

Mrs Graziano said this was her nineteenth year coming to Hardscrabble Farms, and she wasn't gonna put up with any nonsense from anybody. Then she had the chaperones go through everyone's bags to make sure nobody was trying to sneak in any junk food or electronics.

A few kids got busted with stuff in their bags. Mike Barrows had a pound of jelly beans in his backpack, and Duane Higgins got caught trying to smuggle in a giant chocolate-chip cookie.

I was really glad I'd left those candy bars back home, but I was a little worried the chaperones might confiscate my baby wipes. Once Mr Jones caught a whiff of my bag, though, he didn't go digging any further.

After that we had lunch, which was hot dogs, baked beans and stuffed peppers. There weren't any other choices, so if you didn't like any of those things you were out of luck.

When lunch was over, the chaperones told us to scrape our leftovers into a giant pot.

I hadn't touched my stuffed pepper, so I dumped the whole thing.

I asked Mr Healey why we put our leftovers into a pot instead of the trash can. He said at Hardscrabble Farms no food goes to waste, and everything we didn't eat for THIS meal is put into a stew for the NEXT one.

He said it was the same way when he came to this camp as a kid, and they still used the exact same pot. That means there could be leftovers from thirty YEARS ago in that thing.

After lunch Mrs Graziano and the female chaperones took the girls to the other side of camp to go to their cabins.

Mom had actually wanted to volunteer as a chaperone last-minute, but she wasn't comfortable leaving Manny with Rodrick and Grandpa. That kind of stinks, though, because she could've fed me inside information from the girls' side of camp.

Us guys stayed back in the cafeteria to get our cabin assignments. Most of the groups were kids who hang out together at school, but each cabin seemed to have ONE kid who didn't belong.

The school must have decided to spread the troublemakers out so there wouldn't be more than one in any cabin.

The only group that had MORE than one troublemaker was Mr Nuzzi's group. But Mr Nuzzi works as a prison guard, so I guess they figured he could handle it.

Since I registered late, I got put with the group of LEFTOVERS, which included Rowley.

I was glad I got assigned to the same cabin as Rowley, but I wasn't happy his FATHER was the chaperone. Mr Jefferson has never really been a big fan of mine, and I wasn't looking forward to being cooped up with him for a whole WEEK.

It was pretty clear whoever had our cabin last didn't bother cleaning up after themselves.

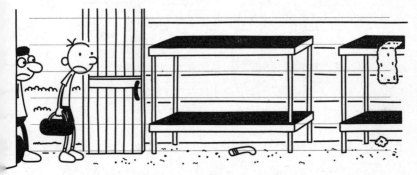

One kid in my group, Julian Trimble, seemed to be taking the situation pretty hard, because his lip started to quiver as soon as we walked through the door.

I was kind of surprised Julian decided to come on this trip, because I'm guessing he's never been away from his parents overnight before.

Julian was always the kid who made a big scene every morning during drop-off time at school. Once, in second grade, he had such a strong grip on his mom that the vice principal had to come down to peel them apart.

I figured Julian decided to go on this trip on his OWN, but when I remembered the scene at the school this morning I started to wonder if his mom had actually tricked him into it.

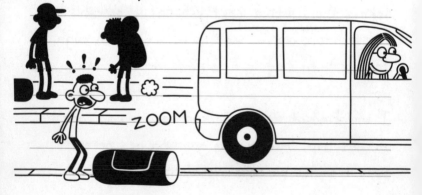

Everybody started picking out their bunks, and that's when I found out why everyone had such big bags.

FLUFF

I had just assumed the bedding would be taken care of, but I guess that was too much to hope for at a place like this.

The closest thing I had to a pillow was my hoodie, which already smelled like Rodrick's ham sandwich.

It was hard finding a mattress without any weird stains on it. I picked a top bunk because I couldn't risk being underneath Julian in case he wet the bed.

Unfortunately, Mr Jefferson slid into the spot right UNDERNEATH me, so now Rowley's dad was my bunkmate.

After we finished unpacking our stuff, we went down to the activities area to do some "team-building" exercises.

The first thing we did was a "trust fall", where one guy would fall backwards and everyone else was supposed to catch him. I guess the point was to show how our teammates have our backs.

But Jordan Lankey did his fall while the rest of us were still working out where to stand.

Mr Jefferson showed us how to form two lines facing each other and then make a "net" by grabbing each other's wrists. So when Jeffrey Swanson got up on the platform we thought we were ready for him.

But Jeffrey is a big boy, and his weight made
Rowley and Gareth Grimes collapse and smash
into each other.

Gareth was missing one of his front teeth, and
everyone got down on their hands and knees to
look for it. Then Emilio Mendoza found the tooth
in Rowley's FOREHEAD.

Mr Jefferson told Emilio to run down and get the
nurse, who brought Gareth a damp washcloth to
stop the bleeding.

But she couldn't pull the tooth out of Rowley's
forehead, because it was really lodged in there.

Mr Jefferson called his wife to come and pick
Rowley up and take him to get it checked out.
I don't know if she ended up going to a doctor
or a dentist, because I have no idea what you
even do for that sort of thing.

So Mr Jefferson was stuck chaperoning a bunch
of kids who weren't HIS. He had us do all these
exercises that were supposed to teach us how to
work together as a team, but all they really did
was show us how BAD we were at it.

We did one activity called the "bucket brigade",
where we had to make a relay line to bring water
from the river all the way to our cabin.

The first guy filled up his bucket and then poured it in the next guy's bucket, and so on.

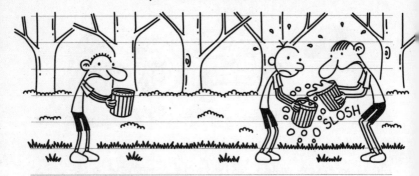

But we spilled so much water along the way that by the time we got to the cabin there was almost nothing left to put in the metal tub we were supposed to fill.

We realized if we were ever gonna finish the activity we needed to find a better way to fill the tub. So we wrung out our sweaty clothes.

After that we did an activity where we had to tie
our wrists together with scarves and go through an
obstacle course made of ropes. But, when it came to
physical activities, our group was pretty hopeless.

After the ropes course, we couldn't untie the scarves because we'd knotted them too tight. And THAT wasn't good, because Timothy Ames needed to use the bathroom in the cabin.

By the end of the day everyone was totally worn out, and I was really glad when Mr Jefferson told us it was time for dinner.

The meal was chicken patties, corn on the cob and stew. I passed on the stew, and I was really glad I did when I saw Jordan pull an entire taco shell out of his bowl. Who KNOWS what year that thing was from.

After dinner we went back to the cabin. Mr Jefferson said that since we had been in the woods we needed to check one another for ticks. Each person was responsible for his bunkmate, which meant I had Mr Jefferson.

But Mr Jefferson's got a lot of hair, and I wasn't gonna go poking through it. For all I knew, there could be a whole COLONY of ticks living in there.

YOU'RE GOOD!

THANKS!

Everybody's always saying how great the outdoors are, but there's all SORTS of creepy-crawlies you need to worry about.

I used to play in the woods all the TIME, until I swallowed a live spider.

But in a place like Hardscrabble Farms there are just as many bugs INSIDE as OUTSIDE. Some sort of beetle burrowed into a kid's ear at dinner, and he had to go to the nurse's station to have it removed.

Jordan found a tick on the back of Julian's neck, and everybody freaked out about it. But Mr Jefferson said Julian would be fine, and he took him down to the nurse.

The second Mr Jefferson and Julian left, the rest of the guys in my cabin went totally NUTS.

I stayed out of everybody's way because I didn't wanna be the fifth person from my group to get seen by the nurse on the first day.

By the time Mr Jefferson got back, the cabin was a wreck and everyone was FILTHY.

I'm guessing nobody has ever cleaned the floors in this place, because when the guys were done rolling around they were covered in dirt and hair.

As a punishment for trashing the cabin, Mr Jefferson made us go to bed EARLY, and he lumped me in with everyone else even though I didn't DO anything. And that's how we ended up going to bed while it was still light out on the first night.

Tuesday
Mr Jefferson woke everybody up at the crack of dawn and said we all needed to take showers before breakfast.

That's when it occurred to me that there wasn't actually a shower in our bathroom. The shower was on the OUTSIDE of the cabin, and the water was in the metal tub we filled up in the bucket brigade yesterday.

I seemed to be the only one who remembered what was IN that tub, because everyone else got in line to take their turn.

Not only was the water UNSANITARY, but apparently it was COLD, too.

I came PREPARED, though. I definitely wasn't gonna be taking any outdoor showers on this trip, but I could still keep myself CLEAN.

Breakfast wasn't a whole lot better than our first two meals, but at least they weren't serving the STEW. The pancakes were hard as ROCKS, though, and they'd break your teeth if you tried to bite through one.

Emilio sneaked a pancake into his pocket so he could mail it home to his mom and show her how bad the food was at camp.

After we cleaned up from breakfast, Mrs Graziano told us the plan for the day.

She said we were gonna do the same types of chores done by kids growing up on farms like this a long time ago.

Mrs Graziano said that in the old days kids worked from the time they got up in the morning until the sun went down. And they had to start working as soon as they were old enough to help their families out.

Which is just ANOTHER reason I'm glad I wasn't alive back then.

My group started off in the barn, and our job was to move bales of hay from one end of the building to the other. It was SERIOUSLY hard, and I have a lot of respect for kids who had to do that kind of work every day.

When we were FINISHED, everybody felt a huge sense of accomplishment.

As we were leaving to move on to the next station, Mr Nuzzi's group came into the barn. He told his team their job was to move the hay bales to the other side, which was where they were to BEGIN with. So don't even ask me why we went to all that trouble.

See, you shouldn't DO that kind of stuff to a kid. When I was in first grade, my teacher told me she was sending me on a "secret mission", and she gave me a note to deliver to another teacher down the hall.

TOP SECRET

And every day after that my teacher handed me
ANOTHER note to deliver.

Well, one day I got curious about what was IN
those notes, and I opened one up. But it was
BLANK inside.

It turns out Mom had told my teacher she was
worried about my "self-esteem", and the whole
secret-mission thing was just a way to make me
feel IMPORTANT. So if anyone wants to know
why I have a hard time taking work seriously
that's how it started.

Our team spent the rest of the morning going
through the other stations. We painted a fence,
repaired a stone wall and stacked firewood outside
the main lodge.

I'll tell you, when I'm older I'm gonna buy a farm of my OWN and set up a camp on the property. Because getting a bunch of kids to work for free and calling it education is GENIUS.

After lunch, when we were heading back to our cabin, Gareth tripped over a rock sticking out of the ground.

When Emilio saw it, he got really upset.

The rock had some scrapes on it, and Emilio said the only person who could've done THAT was Silas Scratch.

Jeffrey said the rock was probably Silas Scratch's
GRAVESTONE, and now we were CURSED
because we had disturbed his resting place.

I tried to talk some sense into these guys. I said
that, first of all, if Silas Scratch was DEAD,
that was good news for everyone. And, second of
all, this COULDN'T be Silas Scratch's gravestone
because he would've had to bury HIMSELF.

I never should've said that, because it just
upset everyone even MORE. Now all of a sudden
Silas Scratch was an UNDEAD farmer who
couldn't be killed.

At dinner, Silas Scratch's "grave" was all anybody could talk about.

Somebody claimed they saw Silas Scratch in the woods. And someone ELSE said they saw him on the other side of camp at the exact same time.

Then Albert Sandy was telling everyone that HE heard Silas Scratch had a network of tunnels beneath the cabins, and that's how he's able to move around so quickly.

So, thanks to Albert Sandy, now kids are too
scared to use the bathrooms at camp.

A few kids said they're just gonna HOLD it until
they get home. That doesn't sound smart to ME,
especially considering we're only on day TWO.

Wednesday
Today, after we finished our farm chores, we had
free time to do whatever we wanted. I decided
I'd just take a nap, but a few of my cabinmates
had other plans.

Gareth, Jeffrey and Jordan said they were sick
of eating STEW for dinner, so they were gonna
go down to the river and catch a FISH.

I thought that was the stupidest idea I'd ever heard, ESPECIALLY since they didn't have a fishing pole or anything like that.

But they were dead serious, and when they headed out I went to the cabin and climbed up into my bunk.

It took me a while to fall asleep, and right when I started to doze off my cabinmates burst through the door.

Believe it or not, those fools had actually managed
to catch a fish. They scooped one right out of
the river using Jeffrey's shirt as a NET.

And, now that they had it, they didn't know
what to DO with it. What was pretty clear was
that no one had any intention of EATING it.

I told the guys if they didn't put the fish in
some water quick it wasn't gonna SURVIVE.

Gareth grabbed the fish by its tail and carried
it to the bathroom, where he put it in the
TOILET. Then Jordan emptied his flask inside
the bowl so the fish had some extra water to flop
around in.

The fish seemed OK for the time being, and I decided to go and get a bucket so we could take the fish back down to the river and let it go.

But, when I went to LEAVE, Mr Jefferson walked into the cabin. The other guys slammed the bathroom door shut, and I tried my best to play it cool.

My guess was that Mr Jefferson wouldn't be too happy about a fish in the toilet, and I didn't wanna get sent to bed early for the second time on this trip.

Mr Jefferson asked me where everyone ELSE was, and I said I thought they might be down by the river. He told me that if I saw anyone I should tell them to come to the main lodge for mail call.

When Mr Jefferson left, we put the lid down on the toilet to make sure the fish didn't flop out onto the floor, then we headed down to the main lodge to join the rest of our class.

Mrs Graziano handed out mail to all the kids who got something delivered from home. Mom sent me a letter, and I'll admit I got a little choked up reading it.

> Dear Gregory,
>
> We miss you so much!
> Can't wait until you're
> back home. Hope you
> are having a <u>wonderful</u>
> time!
>
> Hugs + kisses,
>
> Mom

I got a letter from Rodrick, too, but I didn't
like HIS as much as Mom's.

> Dear Greg,
>
> I found your candy
> bars. Here, you can
> smell the wrappers.
>
> Har, har, har.

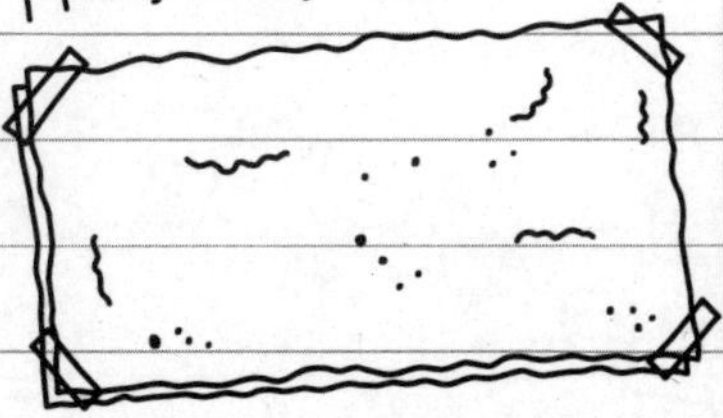

I didn't get a letter from Dad, but I DID get one from the PIG. I just hope someone in my family wrote it as a joke, because if that thing has somehow learned how to write, then I don't even know what to say.

Julian got a letter from home, too. But his mom made a HUGE mistake by sending a photo along with it.

Julian wasn't the ONLY one who seemed homesick. A couple of kids didn't get anything at all, and they asked some of us who DID get letters to read them out loud.

I MADE A BATCH OF YOUR FAVOURITE COOKIES AND PUT THEM IN THE FRIDGE FOR WHEN YOU GET HOME! LOVE, MOM.

A few kids got care packages with fresh clothes and stuff like that.

But the big winner in our group was Graham Bertran, who got a HUGE box that was packed with a ton of supplies.

Back at the cabin later on, we found out Graham had mailed the box to HIMSELF before the trip started, and he had hidden all SORTS of goodies in with the camping supplies.

Luckily, he was willing to SHARE. I never thought I'd eat Doritos out of a hiking boot, but by that point I'd already given up my last shred of dignity.

Emilio looked out of the window and saw Mr Jefferson coming back to the cabin, so we hid all of Graham's stuff under a blanket.

When Mr Jefferson entered the cabin, he walked right by without even noticing.

Unfortunately, we were so focused on the snacks that we forgot all about the FISH.

I feel a little bad for Mr Jefferson, but it was a good reminder to me that you should ALWAYS check inside the toilet before sitting down.

Mr Jefferson was mad and thought this was some kind of practical joke.

And of course he thought I was the guy who came up with it.

So tonight, while the rest of the group was having s'mores and singing songs by the campfire with Mrs Graziano, I was stuck in the cabin with an angry chaperone.

Thursday
Most kids at camp were cruising right along until yesterday, but after those letters from home came it seemed like everyone hit a WALL.

A lot of my classmates are homesick, and they've been asking if they can go back early. But the chaperones say the only way we can go home is if there's some sort of MEDICAL reason.

Well, they shouldn't have put that into people's heads, because now kids are trying to get sick on PURPOSE.

Melinda Henson was acting really strange at lunch. It turns out she ate three servings of stew to make herself sick, which seemed a little extreme to ME.

But after spending a few hours down at the nurse's station with indigestion Melinda was sent back to rejoin her group.

Julian took it one step FURTHER. Mr Jefferson found him in the cabin clutching his stomach next to a half-eaten stick of deodorant.

So that was the end of the road for Julian.

A few hours later Julian's mother arrived to pick him up. But by the time they drove away he seemed to have made a full recovery.

A lot of boys started talking about how Julian had the right idea, and the chaperones caught wind of it.

The next thing we knew, the chaperones were going around collecting everyone's deodorant so no one could follow in Julian's footsteps.

That's bad news for OUR cabin because, with the wet towels and dirty clothes all over the place, and kids showering with sweat water, our cabin ALREADY smells like a monkey house.

The deodorant was probably the one thing keeping the fumes in our cabin from reaching toxic levels.

And if we get sick we're ALL going home early.

That might be OK for everyone ELSE, but it's not all right for ME. Because the sooner I go home, the sooner I have to face DAD.

Saturday
To be honest with you, I had forgotten all about Rowley until he returned to camp yesterday morning.

But when he caught a whiff of our cabin I bet he wished he had just stayed home.

It turns out Rowley got an infection from Gareth's tooth, and that's why he was gone for so long. Rowley brought the tooth WITH him, but I'm not sure what Gareth's supposed to do with it at this point.

Rowley was coming back at an awkward time. We've all been preparing for the last night of the trip, which we have to spend OUTDOORS.

I'm kind of looking forward to it, because that's ONE night we won't have to stay in our stinky cabin.

But I'm not sure my group can even SURVIVE sleeping out in the elements.

We're supposed to build a shelter and a fire tomorrow night, and I have no IDEA how we're supposed to pull THAT off.

Mr Jefferson has been trying to teach us how to do some basic outdoorsy things, but it turns out he's just about as useless as the REST of us.

Yesterday he was trying to teach us how to build a fire, and he broke the "no electronics" rule by using his phone to look up how to do it. But his battery died when a couple of my cabinmates got hold of it to watch videos of screaming goats.

I guess Mr Jefferson learned a LITTLE bit before the battery died, because he got a fire going and told the rest of us to get some kindling. Nobody knew what kindling WAS, though, so we brought back everything we thought might burn.

Rowley came back with what looked like a bunch of
WEEDS and threw them on the fire, but that
totally smothered it.

It turns out the stuff Rowley put on the fire
was actually POISON IVY, and this morning he
woke up covered in spots. Mr Jefferson must've
inhaled the fumes and got it in his LUNGS,
because he was having trouble breathing.

The nurse called Mrs Jefferson to come and pick them both up, and I think they're done for GOOD.

That means my group is the only one without a chaperone. I've heard Mrs Graziano is scrambling to find a replacement, but no dads are willing to give up the rest of their weekend to come out here.

This is really bad timing, because it's supposed to RAIN tomorrow night, and we haven't even started building our shelter. I tried to spy on a group that has a bunch of Boy Scouts in it to see if I could pick up any pointers, but those guys weren't willing to give away their secrets.

While we were off trying to set up our camp, some other group raided our cabin. I guess they must've heard about Graham's snacks, because his stash was totally picked clean.

The thieves also went through MY bag and found the baby wipes, which they used up in our bathroom. They must've tried to flush them down the toilet, because now it was CLOGGED.

The worst part was that the toilet overflowed, and the water ran along the floor in a path from the bathroom to my duffel bag.

DRIP

Everything I owned was wet except for Grandpa's book, which the thieves had tossed onto a bed.

I was really MAD. But when I started flipping through the pages I realized the guys who raided our cabin might've done us a huge FAVOUR.

The book had a ton of useless stuff in it, like a chapter on how to make a working radio out of household objects.

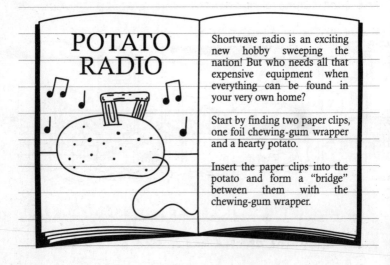

POTATO RADIO

Shortwave radio is an exciting new hobby sweeping the nation! But who needs all that expensive equipment when everything can be found in your very own home?

Start by finding two paper clips, one foil chewing-gum wrapper and a hearty potato.

Insert the paper clips into the potato and form a "bridge" between them with the chewing-gum wrapper.

But there was a lot of GOOD stuff in there, too. There was a chapter on how to identify poison ivy, which would've come in handy yesterday. There were chapters on OTHER outdoorsy things, like how to start a fire without matches, which was great, because Mr Jefferson used all of ours up.

I couldn't wait to try out some of the tips and see if they actually WORKED. I led my group out to our campsite and asked to borrow Emilio's glasses, and I focused a beam of sunlight through a lens onto a dry leaf, the way it said to do in the book. Sure enough, the leaf started smoking and eventually caught fire.

Everyone was excited that we could make a fire without the help of an adult, but we got a little carried away with the high fives and Emilio's glasses got crushed in the celebration.

Apparently Emilio is blind as a bat without his glasses, so the rest of the trip might be a little challenging for him.

Luckily, Jeffrey wears glasses, too, so we can make another fire tomorrow.

When we got back to our cabin after dinner, we got a cold splash of reality. The flooded toilet added to the overall bad smell in our cabin, which by now was TOTALLY overpowering.

We mopped up the floor with our dirty clothes, then put them in a couple of trash bags. But that STILL didn't do the trick.

The WORST smell seemed to be coming from US. And the only way to deal with THAT problem was with deodorant.

Jordan said maybe we should raid one of the girls' cabins and steal some of THEIR deodorant, but that turned into a big debate about whether girls actually USE deodorant.

But what everyone was excited about was the idea of going on a RAID.

The person who was MOST excited was Emilio. But we told him it was too dangerous for him to go with us since he couldn't SEE.

He said we NEEDED him because he has an excellent sense of smell and could sniff out the girls' cabins. We weren't sure if he was bluffing, so we ran him through a smell test where he had to identify a bunch of different things. And, sure enough, he got every single one.

So Emilio was in. We all started getting ready, but right when we were about to head out Mr Nuzzi came to check on us.

I guess it was pretty obvious to Mr Nuzzi that we were up to no good, so he told us we'd all be in BIG trouble if he caught any of us sneaking out. Plus, he heard Silas Scratch was on the prowl tonight so we'd better stay indoors.

Then Mr Nuzzi left, and a few minutes later he came back with a bottle of talcum powder.

He sprinkled it in a big circle round our cabin so that, if we DID leave, our footprints would give us away.

SHAKE
SHAKE

Everyone started to panic because they thought we were trapped in our cabin for the rest of the night. But then I remembered a chapter from my BOOK that could help us.

☾ HIDING YOUR NUMBERS

Ancient ninjas had a clever way of fooling their enemies.

When travelling in a group, ninjas would walk in single file, carefully stepping into the same set of footprints.

Then they'd ambush their pursuers, who would be shocked to discover that they were not following the tracks of ONE person but many!

Mr Nuzzi had left his OWN footprints in the talcum powder when he was spreading it around. So all we needed to do was follow in his exact footsteps and he'd never know we left.

The only problem was that Mr Nuzzi's footprints were a lot bigger than any of ours. But Mr Jefferson had left his hiking boots under the bed, and they looked like a perfect match.

I went first. It was a little hard staying in Mr Nuzzi's tracks, but I made it to the other side of the talcum powder.

Then I tossed the boots back to the NEXT guy.

We got everyone out of the cabin that way. Even Emilio, who hitched a ride with Jeffrey.

Once we were all clear, we headed through the woods towards the girls' cabins. But, before we knew it, we were totally lost. It was kind of scary because nobody even knew which way OUR cabin was.

Then Jeffrey made everything a hundred times WORSE by bringing up the subject of Silas Scratch. Jeffrey said Silas Scratch was probably watching our every move and was gonna pick us off one by one and eat us alive.

That got my cabinmates all stirred up, and I thought they were gonna scatter in every direction.

But Emilio saved the day when he picked up a scent in the air.

He said he could smell a girls' cabin and it wasn't that far off.

Sure enough, one of the cabins was about fifty feet away. We crept up as quietly as we could, then put some of our team-building skills into action to get up to an open window.

It sounded like everyone was asleep inside. So I lowered myself through the window and dropped down to the floor without making a sound.

But when I looked around I realized I was in a cabin full of GIRL SCOUTS.

I decided to call off the mission to get the deodorant, but by then it was already too late.

Everything after THAT is kind of a blur. I remember girls yelling, hands grabbing at my ankles, and my cabinmates trampling one another to get out of the front door.

Then it was just a mad dash through the woods.

Don't ask me HOW, but we found our way back to our cabin. Unfortunately, we forgot all about the talcum powder, and we totally trampled it. But at that point it was the LEAST of our worries.

I thought the mission was a total failure, but it turns out we didn't come back empty-handed. Graham had swiped a bag at the girls' cabin and brought it with him.

I definitely wasn't comfortable with STEALING and said that one of us needed to sneak the bag back to the girls' cabin before anyone noticed it was missing.

But I got outvoted on that idea because everyone else was curious to see what was inside.

The clothes in the bag didn't look like they belonged to any girls OUR age.

But, by the time we figured out who the bag actually BELONGED to, the owner was standing in our doorway.

I thought Mrs Graziano found us because of the talcum powder, but it turns out it was even easier for her than THAT. As soon as she opened her cabin door, she found Emilio stumbling around in the dark. Which just goes to show, you should never leave a man behind.

Mrs Graziano chewed us out for our "immature shenanigans". She said we couldn't be trusted on our own for the night, so she was gonna get on the phone and find an emergency chaperone.

I couldn't imagine who would be willing to drive all the way out to this place in the middle of the night, but I knew that WHOEVER it was he wasn't gonna be HAPPY about it.

And it turns out I was right.

Sunday

I really wish Mrs Graziano had just sent me
HOME instead of calling Dad to chaperone us
for the last day. Dad was already mad ENOUGH
about the CAR, and now he had to babysit a
bunch of unshowered middle-schoolers.

And it wasn't fun breaking the news to him that
we didn't even have a working bathroom in our cabin.

I figured I owed it to Dad to at least give him
a basic rundown of the camp, but he seemed to
already know everything I tried to tell him.
Somehow he even knew about the STEW, because
when somebody put a serving on his plate he
scraped it right back into the pot.

At first I thought Dad must've been a chaperone when RODRICK went to this place, but when I saw one of the other chaperones greet Dad I put it all together.

WELCOME BACK, FRANK!

SMACK

Dad went to Hardscrabble Farms when he was MY age.

No WONDER he wasn't happy to be here. If his experience was anything like MINE, I'm sure he never imagined in a million years that he'd be BACK.

Me and my cabinmates spent the day trying to set up our camp for the overnighter. And it was pretty clear Dad had no intention of helping out.

Half the time he was off somewhere else doing who knows what. And when he WAS around he didn't lift a finger.

So we set up our shelter without him. Luckily, Grandpa's book had a chapter on how to build a waterproof lean-to, so we didn't NEED Dad's help.

At dinner some kids from another group seemed really shaken up. They said they were gathering firewood and came across an old shack that they were 99% sure belonged to Silas Scratch.

This is where I was hoping Dad would tell everyone Silas Scratch was just a made-up story to keep kids from leaving their cabins at night. But he DIDN'T.

He said that when HE went to Hardscrabble Farms a couple of kids went poking around Silas Scratch's shack and were never heard from AGAIN.

That was the WORST thing Dad could've said just before we were supposed to spend the night in the woods.

After dinner, Mrs Graziano told everyone to get whatever they needed from their cabins and bring it to their campsites.

A bunch of kids were begging to sleep INSIDE, but Mrs Graziano said this is how it's always been on the last night at Hardscrabble Farms, and it's the way it's always gonna be.

We had got the fire started earlier, and when we got to our campsite it was still going. The fire was dying down, though, so we needed to get more wood to feed it. But, once it got DARK out, the guys in my group were too scared to leave the fire to help me collect sticks.

I would've asked DAD for help, but who KNOWS where he was.

So I went to look for firewood by myself. The area around our campsite was picked pretty clean of sticks, so I had to go deeper into the woods. But I got all turned around, and I couldn't remember which way our campsite was.

I started to panic a little, but then I saw a
light that I thought must be our campfire. I
headed towards it, and when I got closer I
couldn't believe where the light was coming from.

I have to admit, I didn't really buy any of the
Silas Scratch stuff until this moment. But now I
thought I might actually die of FEAR.

Something about that light didn't look right,
though. I thought it was coming from a fireplace
inside the shack, but it was actually from a
LIGHT BULB. It didn't make a lot of sense
to me that a crazy farmer who eats slugs and
berries had ELECTRICITY.

The door on the front of the place was barred shut. So I walked round the back, and there was a metal door that was unlocked.

I held my breath and pushed it open, then I stepped inside. My heart was practically beating out of my chest, but I HAD to know what was in there.

When I saw what was inside, I realized this place wasn't a shack at ALL. It was some sort of maintenance shed with a bunch of tools, and they didn't even look that OLD.

I went a little further in. When I walked down a hallway, I found something that REALLY shocked me.

It was a BATHROOM, with a toilet and a sink and EVERYTHING. There were even a few rolls of extra toilet paper, and it wasn't the CHEAP stuff, either.

My head was spinning at that point. I was ready to run back to our campsite and tell everyone what I'd found, when I heard something that sent shivers down my spine.

It was the sound of WHISTLING, and it was coming from right BEHIND me.

I turned to run, and that's when I ran smack into DAD.

I was totally speechless. I couldn't understand what he was doing taking a shower in a maintenance shed, but then he started talking.

Dad said when HE went to Hardscrabble Farms the bathroom situation was even WORSE than it is now.

There was only one outhouse, which everyone at the camp shared.

There was no shower, and if you wanted to get clean you had to go down to the river with a bar of soap.

Then one day when Dad was collecting firewood he found this maintenance shed that was used for keeping up the property during the off-season.

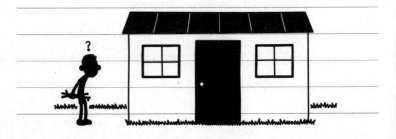

When he realized there was a toilet and a shower inside, he knew he had to keep it a secret or EVERYONE would find out.

So he came up with the story of Silas Scratch to throw the other kids off the trail.

Dad said when he got here yesterday he was pretty surprised the Silas Scratch thing was still going after all these years. But he figured he'd just go with it so he could keep the bathroom to himself.

I was pretty mad at Dad for causing everyone all this stress. But I have to admit that coming up with a crazy story to protect a secret bathroom is EXACTLY the kind of thing I'd do MYSELF.

I realized I'd been away from the campsite for a while and my cabinmates probably thought I got snatched up by Silas Scratch.

So I asked Dad to help me find my way back to the campsite.

It had started to rain, and by the time we got back the fire was completely OUT. I guess my group got desperate and threw in anything that would burn, because I found my BOOK in there. Or at least what was left of it.

My cabinmates had picked apart our shelter for firewood, and that's where me and Dad found them, all huddled together.

I really didn't wanna spend the night out in the rain, and thankfully Dad didn't, EITHER.

I guess he wasn't too concerned about the camp rules, because he sneaked us all back into our cabin. It might've stunk to high heaven in there, but it was the best night of sleep I've had in my life.

Monday

This morning we packed up all our stuff and brought it to the parking lot.

Almost everyone in my class looked like a WRECK from sleeping out in the woods overnight, but MY group actually looked REFRESHED.

My cabinmates kept saying how LUCKY we were to have survived the week with Silas Scratch prowling around. And it was all I could do to bite my tongue.

Believe me, I was tempted to tell everyone that Silas Scratch was a hoax. People might've even treated me like a HERO for finally putting an end to the whole thing.

But I figured I might get stuck chaperoning at this place one day, and if I do I'll wanna use that bathroom MYSELF.

SMACK

I was about to load my bag onto the bus, but then Dad told me I could ride home with HIM. That was WAY better than sitting in someone's lap, so I took Dad up on his offer.

On the way out, there was a bus coming in with a whole new crop of kids. I quickly scribbled a message to warn them about what they were in for. I figured it was the LEAST I could do.

BEWARE OF SILAS SCRATCH

ACKNOWLEDGEMENTS

Thanks to my amazing family for cheering me on and for bringing so much joy to my life.

Thanks to Charlie Kochman for your dogged commitment to making sure every Wimpy Kid book is all that it can be. Thanks to the team at Abrams, including Michael Jacobs, Jason Wells, Veronica Wasserman, Susan Van Metre, Jen Graham, KeriLee Horan, Chad W. Beckerman, Alison Gervais, Elisa Garcia, Erica La Sala and Kim Ku.

Thanks to Shaelyn Germain and Anna Cesary for helping to create an amazing building from the ground up in the midst of all of our commitments. Thanks to Deb Sundin and the staff at An Unlikely Story for bringing a great independent bookstore into the world.

Thanks to Rich Carr and Andrea Lucey for your unbelievable support throughout the years. Thanks to Paul Sennott and Ike Williams for your invaluable advice.

Thanks to Jess Brallier for being a friend and mentor to me for the past fifteen years. Thanks to everyone at Poptropica for your support and inspiration.

Thanks to Sylvie Rabineau for your continued guidance and friendship. Thanks to Keith Fleer for all of your help. Thanks to everyone in Hollywood who is working to bring new Wimpy Kid stories to life, including Nina Jacobson, Brad Simpson, Elizabeth Gabler, Roland Poindexter, Ralph Milero and Vanessa Morrison.

ABOUT THE AUTHOR

Jeff Kinney is a #1 *New York Times* bestselling author and a five-time Nickelodeon Kids' Choice Award winner for Favourite Book. Jeff has been named one of *Time* magazine's 100 Most Influential People in the World. He is also the creator of Poptropica, which was named one of *Time* magazine's 50 Best Websites. He spent his childhood in the Washington, D.C., area and moved to New England in 1995. Jeff lives with his wife and two sons in Massachusetts, where they own a bookstore, An Unlikely Story.